For Alan
~ *M.P.*

For Megan
~ *J.M.*

Published in 1997 by Magi Publications
22 Manchester Street, London W1M 5PG

Text © 1997 Maggie Pearson
Illustrations © 1997 Joanne Moss

Maggie Pearson and Joanne Moss have asserted their rights
to be identified as the author and illustrator of this
work under the Copyright, Designs and Patents Act, 1988.

Printed and bound in Hong Kong

ISBN 1 85430 412 7

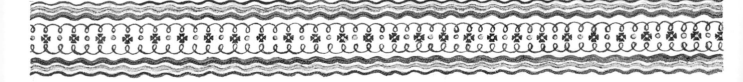

TALES
from
NEAR *and* FAR

Retold by Maggie Pearson
illustrated by Joanne Moss

MAGI PUBLICATIONS
London

Introduction

In every land, since time began, people have told one another stories. To people without television or films, or even books, the storyteller was, and still is, in many countries, a very important person. He is a magician, using only words to conjure up a whole new world and people it with brave and clever heroes and heroines; with fools and tricksters, with talking animals and stranger creatures still. It is a world where a boy can soar on raven's wings, and a foolish king will take advice from a sensible little girl. Some stories, like the story of the great rain, are found the world over, because floods happen everywhere at some time or another. But the people of West Africa, who took their tales of Anansi to the Caribbean with them, must have been very surprised to find French settlers there, telling similar stories about a character called Raynard the fox. These days it is hard to tell which stories began with Raynard and which with Anansi. You will not find any of the best-known stories in this collection – no Cinderella, no Little Red Riding Hood – but there may be one or two you already know – or think you do. There is no *right* way of telling these stories.

My father was a storyteller. The most magical part of each day was just before I fell asleep, when he told me my bedtime story. Though he told some of them many times over, he never told them exactly the same way twice.

That is how storytelling works: sometimes the storyteller changes something; sometimes the listener notices something new. It is all about sharing. These stories I have gathered I now share with you. Take them with you, and share them also.

Maggie Pearson

Contents

The Face in the Mirror   9

The Snow Child   12

Anansi and the Scarecrow   17

The Pied Piper   22

The Field of Ragwort   28

Raven Boy   33

The Terrible Dibdib   38

The Great Rain   43

The Big White Cat   48

Stone Soup   53

The Smallest Boy in the World   58

The King with Dusty Feet   64

The Fox and the Rooster   69

A Song for Hinemoa   74

The Face in the Mirror

Chinese

Look in any mirror, and what do you see? Your own face, of course. You know it is. But what would you think if you had never seen a mirror before? Long, long ago, there lived a man who owned the only mirror in the world. How he came by it I don't know, but from that day on, he was never happy again, for that mirror told lies. It kept telling him he was getting older. He knew that this wasn't so. He could see his friends growing older, but he was still the same young man that he had always been. Wasn't he?

Yet every time he looked in the mirror, it showed another grey hair, another wrinkle.

The man shut the mirror away in an old tin chest, and never looked at it again. But, of course, he still continued to grow older, as people do. And as old men do, at last he died.

Some days later his son was sorting through his father's things and came across the old tin chest. He opened it and looked inside.

What did he see?

He saw the mirror, but as no one had ever seen one before, he exclaimed:

"Why, it's a picture of my father as a young man! How surprised he looks, to be having his picture painted!"

He sighed, and looked sad. "I do miss him so."

Wonder of wonders! The face gazing back at him was suddenly sad, too.

"Why, that almost looks like a tear running down my father's cheek," said the son.

Every time he opened the old tin box, his father's face seemed to share his feelings, his smiles, his tears and his moments of thoughtfulness.

He was careful to keep it a secret, especially from his wife. If he told her about the magical picture, she would be bound to tell her mother and after that, the whole town would know, and they would all want to have a peep.

"What's that?" asked his wife, coming into the room suddenly.

The young man shut the lid quickly. "It's just a picture of my father as a young man – *you* wouldn't want to see it."

But she did. One day, when her husband was out, she opened the old tin chest and looked inside.

What did she see? She saw the mirror!

"Oh," she exclaimed. "He has a picture of another woman!"

She burst into tears and sobbed and screamed so loudly that her mother came running to see what the matter was.

"He's in love with another woman!" shrieked the wife.

"Surely not!"

"He is! He keeps her picture in that old tin chest."

Slowly the mother opened the lid.

What did she see? She saw the mirror.

"This old hag!" she cried. "He can't be in love with her. She's older than I am!"

"Then why did he lie to me? He said it was a picture of his father."

Poor young man! The moment he came home, his wife and her mother pounced on him, both shouting at once, so that it was some time before he realised they were talking about the picture in the old tin chest.

"This?" he cried. "What's the matter with you? It's just a picture of my father

when he was a young man."

"Oooh! How can you say that, when we can see the truth for ourselves?"

Then they were all off again:

"Young man!"

"Young woman!"

"Old woman!"

Each time one of them looked in the box, they knew they were right and the others wrong, and they shouted all the louder, until a gentle voice from the window asked:

"What are you all doing, making such a fuss?"

A little old man was standing there, looking in. "How sad my old friend would be to hear his family squabbling so."

"You're my father's dearest friend!" exclaimed the young man. "You remember how he looked when he was young, don't you?"

"Of course. May I see?"

The son pushed the chest towards the window and the little old man looked inside.

What did he see? He saw the mirror.

He smiled. "Oh yes, this is a picture of my friend, but not as a young man. It must have been painted towards the end of his life. Such happy memories it brings back!"

"Then keep it," cried the young man. "Keep it to remember him by."

"Yes, yes," the wife and her mother agreed. "We don't want it. Take it away!"

"Thank you, I will," the old man said.

He took the mirror home with him, and it never gave him anything but happiness for the rest of his days.

The Snow Child

Russian

One winter's day, Old Peter carved a child from snow. He made it out of love for his wife, Anna, because they had no children. It was a little girl with a turned-up nose, smiling mouth and dimples in her cheeks. The next day their Snow Child had gone, leaving a trail of small footprints in the snow. Peter called the dog, and followed the footprints right down to the village. Soon he came running back.

"Anna, Anna, come and see!"

For there was the Snow Child, playing with all the other children, laughing, and tumbling, and throwing snowballs.

"She's a real child," cried Anna. "Our very own child! Let's cook a meal to celebrate!"

She called the Snow Child in from play.

"Come into the warm and eat your dinner," she said.

But the Snow Child stood in the doorway, and two big tears rolled down her cheeks.

"I cannot eat your food," she said. "If I come inside, I shall melt."

So Peter carved a little chair and table of snow, with a bowl of snow-fruit and a snow-cup full of frozen water.

By bedtime he had made her a little bed of snow to sleep on. And when Anna and Peter went outside into the cold to kiss her goodnight, she said:

"How much do you love me?"

"More than anything else in the world," said Anna.

"Then I'll stay with you," said the Snow Child.

All winter the Snow Child played with the other children, sliding downhill, faster than the wind, dancing across the ice, lighter than a snowflake. She was the best at hide-and-seek, because she was the same colour as the snow she hid in.

One day, the children couldn't find her at all, and thought she must have gone home.

So they went home, too, in ones and twos. And the Snow Child was left all alone.

Which way was home? This way? That way? She was quite lost.

She asked a bird.

"Which way is home, bird? Do you know?"

"Home!" squawked the bird, and the Snow Child followed it. Soon they came to a tree, deep in the forest. The bird settled high in the branches.

"Home!" it squawked again.

"It's home for you, bird, but not for me," said the Snow Child sadly.

She saw a rabbit, scratching its ears.

"Do you know the way home, rabbit?"

The rabbit looked at her, and ran off. The Snow Child followed it, until it disappeared down a hole in the ground.

"That's home for you, rabbit, but not for me. Can't anyone tell me the way to my home?"

"I can," said a fox. "I can find my way blindfolded to Old Peter's house by the smell of those plump chickens he keeps."

"Then take me home, please," pleaded the Snow Child.

"What will you give me if I do?"

"I know Old Peter and Anna love me more than anything else in the world. They will be so pleased to see me that they will give you anything you ask."

"I don't ask for much," said the fox. "Just one of those plump chickens for my dinner. It's been a long, hard winter."

So off they set towards home.

And of course Peter and Anna were pleased to see her, but when the Snow Child told them about the fox, and how he had asked for one of their plump chickens, Anna cried:

"The cheek of it!"

"After I've spent so much time and trouble keeping them safe from him!" agreed Old Peter. Between them, they secretly decided to put the dog in the basket instead. They covered it with a cloth, and the Snow Child gave it to the fox.

Off trotted the fox, very pleased, with the basket in his mouth. Out of the basket leapt the dog, snapping and snarling. He chased the fox all the way back to the forest.

And the Snow Child began to cry.

"Never mind," said Anna. "You are safe now."

"I was safe with the fox," sobbed the Snow Child. "He brought me home. I'm crying because you said you loved me more than anything else in the world, but you don't love me enough to give away one chicken to have me back again."

"But we *do* love you!"

"Not as much as one of your plump chickens!" And the Snow Child went on crying and crying until she was nearly all tears, with just a flurry of snowflakes

15

in the middle. And the wind came and carried her away.

Every winter Old Peter carves a little chair and table and a bed out of snow. He carves dishes of food, and flowers and toys, but he never carves another child.

There is only one Snow Child.

Sometimes they hear her voice, singing in the wind.

Sometimes they see her in the dancing snowflakes.

Sometimes they think they hear her tapping on the window.

They open the door, but there's no one there.

Some day they hope that she'll come back. Because now they know that they *do* love her more than all of their plump chickens. More than anything else in the world.

Anansi and the Scarecrow

West Indian

Anansi, he's tricky. Anansi, he's so sharp, he wants to be careful he doesn't cut himself some day. Anansi was a farmer. All day, he worked in his vegetable patch, digging and sowing and reaping and hoeing, while his wife and little ones stayed at home.

One day, Anansi said to himself: "Why do I have to work so hard, while Mrs Anansi just lazes at home all day?"

Mrs Anansi might have had something to say about that, if she had heard him. All he had to do was grow their food. She had to cook and clean and sew, fetch water from the well, find wood for the fire and keep an eye on the children.

Anansi went on: "If it wasn't for Mrs Anansi and the little ones eating all the food I grow, I could sell it in the market. I'd be a rich man in no time. Then I could laze around all day and pay someone else to do the work."

But how was he going to get rid of his wife and children?

Anansi, he's smart.

He ate a whole mouthful of hot peppers, so the sweat was streaming down his face. Then he went home and said to his wife: "I don't feel well."

"You've been working too long in the hot sun," she said. "Just you lie down and take it easy until dinnertime."

So he did.

Dinnertime came and dinner smelt good, but Anansi said he wasn't hungry.

"All the more for us," said Mrs Anansi cheerfully.

Next morning, Anansi took ashes from the fireplace and smeared them over his skin to make himself look pale.

"I still don't feel well," he said. "I think perhaps I'm dying."

Breakfast smelt good and dinner even better, but Anansi lay on his bed and wouldn't eat.

"I'm dying," he said. "Tomorrow I'll be dead for sure."

He didn't think he could go on any longer than that without a taste of his wife's delicious cooking.

"When I die," said Anansi the next day, "don't bury me in the cold, dark earth. Just lay me down in the vegetable patch and cover me over with fresh, green branches. Then take yourselves off, far, far away, so that you don't catch this terrible illness that's struck me down."

Then Anansi gave a sort of gurgle, and shut his eyes.

Mrs Anansi and the children listened to his tummy rumbling for a bit, and when that stopped, Mrs Anansi said: "He's dead."

She held a mirror up to his mouth. Anansi held his breath, so he wouldn't mist up the mirror.

"Yes, he's dead for sure," said Mrs Anansi. Then, weeping and crying, they all carried him out to the vegetable patch and laying him down, covered him over with fresh, green branches, just as he'd told them to do. Then they packed up their things, and off they went.

As soon as he was sure they had gone, Anansi pushed off the branches, stood

up, and went to see if there was any stew left. There was, just a little, and it was delicious. But after that, he had to cook for himself. And fetch the water, and the wood. Without his wife and children to feed, Anansi had more vegetables to sell. He took them to a market a long way off, so he wouldn't meet anyone he knew, but he reckoned it was worth it.

A year went by. Anansi was doing well, but Mrs Anansi and the children, they were close to starving.

"After a whole year, the germs must be gone," thought Mrs Anansi. "I'll go and put some fresh, green branches over my poor Anansi."

She hurried back home, and what did she find? Someone had been working the vegetable patch! Someone had been harvesting the vegetables and carrying them all off to market! Now Mrs Anansi, she wasn't Mrs Anansi for nothing. Like her husband, she knew a trick or two. She would catch the thief and make him pay for what he had stolen from her poor, starving children.

She made a scarecrow out of straw. She covered the straw with clay, and she covered the clay with sticky tar, and left the scarecrow standing up among the vegetables.

Late that night Anansi came home from market, money jingling in his pocket. He saw the figure of a man standing in his vegetable patch.

"Hey, you, get out of there!" cried Anansi.

The figure didn't move. It still didn't move when Anansi strode up to it, and punched it in the face.

His fist stuck fast to the tar.

"Let go of me!" shouted Anansi, punching with his other fist, which stuck as fast as the first.

"Let go, or I'll kick you!" yelled Anansi, and he did. Twice. Twice was all he could manage, before his feet were stuck, too.

That didn't stop Anansi from using his head. When Mrs Anansi turned up in the morning with all the neighbours to catch the thief, there was her own husband, stuck fast from his head to his toes.

"Serves you right!" she said. "Serves you right, Anansi, for leaving us to starve."

"What about you?" yelled Anansi. "Burying me without being certain-sure I was dead!"

The neighbours helped Mrs Anansi to pull him free, then they left them both to make it up.

Anansi was sick of cooking and cleaning and fetching and carrying. He had missed the children, too. As for his wife, well, she had known what Anansi was like before she married him.

"But if you ever try that trick again," she said, "I'll make certain-sure you're dead. I'll bury you three metres underground next time!"

The Pied Piper

German

Nobody saw the coming of him. He appeared out of thin air, or so it seemed. Into thin air he vanished again, when his work was done. No one even knew his name, so they called him the Pied Piper, from the ragged red and yellow coat he wore and the curiously-carved flute that hung around his neck.

It all began with the rats. Every town has its rats, lurking in drains and rubbish dumps, creeping out after dark. But Hamelin was overrun with them, gangs of them, scampering down the streets in broad daylight, as if they owned the place. Shut the door, and they would come in through the windows. Shut the windows and they would scamper up the drainpipe and creep in under the eaves. Very soon, the townsfolk began to mutter and grumble:

"Why isn't the Council doing something about it?"

"What do we pay them for?"

"Not just to eat big dinners and drive around in fancy carriages. Oh no!"

The Mayor and the City Council liked to think that was what they *were* paid for. But they would not be able to do it for much longer if they couldn't find a way of getting rid of those rats. They tried everything – rat catchers, rat poison, rat traps, nippy little terriers and big fat cats. They might as well have tried to drain the River Weser with a teaspoon.

Then someone suggested that they offer a reward.

"A reward!" the Mayor repeated thoughtfully.

In the street outside, the air trembled for a moment, as if a curtain had been pushed aside.

The Mayor was still thinking aloud. "A reward! Let someone else solve the problem – and we take the credit!"

Then came a gentle knock at the door. Before anyone could say "Come in", the door swung open of its own accord, and in walked the Pied Piper, beanpole-thin, with a voice like the whispering of autumn leaves.

"Did someone mention a reward?" he said.

"A reward – er –" stammered the Mayor.

"For ridding you of those rats?"

"Can you do it?"

"Oh yes," said the Pied Piper.

"You really can get rid of every one?"

"Every one. One thousand pounds is my price."

"One thousand pounds!" The Mayor's face split into a smile. "My dear sir, we would pay fifty thousand!"

"No you wouldn't," said the Pied Piper. "Not once the job was done. But I won't take a penny less than a thousand. If that's understood, then I'll begin."

"A thousand it is," replied the Mayor.

The Pied Piper strolled out into the street again. A ghost of a smile was on his face as he raised the pipe to his lips and began to play. Such a sad, sweet tune it was, that people stopped to listen. And standing there listening, they heard another sound besides the music – a whispering and a squeaking and a pattering of tiny feet. Rats! Out of the doorways they came scuttling, down from the windows they hopped, and down from under the roofs they tumbled in their haste not to be left behind.

Down the street the Pied Piper strode, playing all the while, and after him came

23

the rats in their hundreds – in their thousands! Like a great, rolling river they scurried along, heads high, eyes closed and noses twitching, as if, just out of sight, they could smell the gates of Paradise, made of pure green cheese.

The Pied Piper came to the river bank, and stepped into a little boat moored there.

Still he played, as the boat danced away over the rippling water. Dancing after it came the rats. Wave after wave of rats fell into the River Weser until not one of them was left alive, and the river carried them away.

"Ring the church bells!" ordered the Mayor. "This is a day to celebrate."

What about the Pied Piper? There he stood, in his ragged coat of red and yellow, with his hand outstretched.

"Ah yes," muttered the Mayor. "The reward. I hadn't forgotten. Fifty pounds, wasn't it?"

"You were willing to offer me fifty thousand," the Pied Piper said softly. "But one thousand was my price and one thousand I am asking. A bargain is a bargain."

"I don't make bargains with people like you," scoffed the Mayor.

The Pied Piper's voice was still quiet – oh deathly quiet!

"I'll have my thousand pounds and be on my way, or you'll hear me pipe a different tune."

Many who heard these words wished the Mayor would give him his money so they could be rid of him, but the Mayor answered:

"You can't frighten me. What will you do? Bring the rats back again? I don't think so! Take the fifty pounds and go, before I set the dogs on you!"

"I'm going," said the Pied Piper. "Keep your fifty pounds. I don't want it."

Once again he stepped into the street, and this time he began to play a tune

that told of childhood dreams, half remembered. While their mothers and fathers stood caught in its spell, all the children of Hamelin gathered in the street, chattering and laughing, as if they were off on holiday. Then, as the Pied Piper moved away, the children began to dance after him. There was no stopping them! Lock the doors, and they climbed out of the windows. Catch their hands, and they just laughed and twisted away. Call after them: "Where are you going? Stop! Don't leave us!" and they paused just long enough to wave goodbye before they were caught up in a great river of children, dancing down the street. Hand in hand they skipped along after the Pied Piper, up and down the streets of Hamelin, then out of the town and into the country. Down the green lanes they went, and over the meadows, and in and out of the forest trees. Fainter and fainter the music grew, until there was a sudden shimmering in the air, like sunlight on still water. Suddenly, everything went quiet.

The townspeople searched the woods and fields, but not one trace of their children could they find, except for one little lame boy, who sat sobbing as if his heart would break at the foot of the mountain they call the Koppelberg.

"Where have all the children gone?" they asked him, and, without speaking, he pointed to the mountain.

"What? Over the mountain? That is impossible in so short a time!"

The boy shook his head. "No," he said. "The children went into the mountain, and it swallowed them up." He had been too lame and slow to follow them. Then he told a strange tale of a magical land where it was always summer, and everyone was young, and no one was ever hungry or lame. He sobbed even louder, as he thought of how he had lost his chance of walking straight on his own two legs.

The Mayor of Hamelin sent out messengers to find the Pied Piper. He offered any reward he would care to name – yes, fifty thousand pounds – if he would bring the children back again. But no messenger could ever find him or the children, or any road that led to that magical land where grown-ups can never go, not even in their dreams.

The Field of Ragwort

Irish

The one-shoemaker, that's the leprechaun, always tap-tap-tapping away at one shoe, and never the other one of the pair to be seen, nor yet the leather to make it with. If you should be walking through the countryside one day, and you hear a tap-tapping, look carefully about you. It may be a woodpecker, searching for insects on the bark of a tree. It may be a thrush, tapping a snail's shell on the ground. But it just could be that you would come across a little mannikin, sitting cross-legged on the ground, tapping away with his hammer, with his shoemaker's last in front of him, and the one shoe on it.

Once you've found him, don't just tiptoe away. Grab him, and hold him fast. For somewhere, not far off, he will have hidden his store of gold, and if you can get him to lead you to it, you would be rich for life.

But he's a tricky one, the leprechaun.

Pat, being an Irishman, knew all about leprechauns. He'd been hearing tales of them since he was a wee, small boy, but he never expected to see one, for all that.

One day, as he was going home from work, he heard a tap-tapping, not far away. And there Pat saw him, the little fellow, banging away at the one shoe on the last in front of him.

Pat knew a thing or two more about leprechauns than I've told you. Lay hold of him you might, but keeping hold of him is another thing altogether. He'll

pinch and he'll punch, and he is as slippery as a nestful of eels.

So what did Pat do? He took off the leprechaun's little green cap, and put it in his pocket, for he knew that if there's one thing a leprechaun prizes more than all the world, it's that little green cap he wears. Outdoors or in, working or playing, eating or sleeping, that cap stays on the leprechaun's head. No one knows why it should be so, but it is.

So when this leprechaun felt a draught about his ears, he leapt up, saw Pat standing there and began to shout.

"Give it back! Give me back my little green cap, or I'll turn you into a toad, so I will." Pat knew he couldn't do that, so he just laughed.

The leprechaun started punching Pat about the knees – which was as high as he could reach. "Give it back!" he yelled. "You thief! You bully!"

"Stop that!" said Pat, "or I'll throw you in the river. What will you give me now, to have it back safely on your head again?"

"Will you take three wishes?" suggested the leprechaun.

Pat shook his head. "I've heard of folks who got three wishes, and by the time they reached the third one, they were wishing they'd never had three wishes in the first place."

"I suppose it's my store of gold you'll be wanting, then?" said the leprechaun, sulkily.

"That's right," said Pat.

"And you'll leave me a beggar, starving and homeless in my old age?" moaned the leprechaun.

"I've never heard of a leprechaun yet, who was starving or homeless. Come on,

show me where you've hidden the gold, and you shall have your cap back."

"You've a heart of stone," said the leprechaun. "But I'll show you. I suppose I couldn't have my cap to wear as we're going along? To save me from getting chilblains on my ears?"

"You could not," said Pat. "I may have a heart of stone but my head's not made of wood! Come on, now. Admit I've beaten you, fair and square, and I've a right to the gold as my reward."

The leprechaun sighed and picked up his work. Off he went, grumbling into his beard, with Pat following along behind him, until they came to a field where nothing but ragwort grew.

"Under the ragwort," said the leprechaun, "that's where it is. Now give me back my cap."

"Which particular ragwort would that be?" asked Pat.

"That one," said the leprechaun, pointing.

"Do I have your word on that?"

"You have." Tricky a leprechaun may be, but he keeps his word, and his word is always the truth.

"I'd better start digging, then," said Pat. "Do you have such a thing as a spade about you?"

"I'm a shoemaker, not a gardener," snapped the leprechaun. "Fetch your own spade. But don't expect me to wait around till you come back. Just give me my cap, and I'll be on my way."

That seemed fair enough to Pat. But to be on the safe side, he tied his handkerchief round the ragwort plant the leprechaun had pointed out to him.

Then he said: "Will you give me your word that you won't touch the plant, or the handkerchief, or what's under the plant?"

"I'll give you my word on that," said the leprechaun.

So Pat gave him back his cap, and in the wink of an eye, the little fellow was 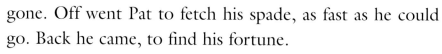 gone. Off went Pat to fetch his spade, as fast as he could go. Back he came, to find his fortune.

There was the ragwort plant, with the handkerchief tied round it. But he had barely begun to dig, when he noticed something flapping in the breeze beside him. It was another handkerchief, tied round another ragwort.

Then he saw another – and another! Every ragwort plant in that field had a handkerchief tied round it. The leprechaun had kept his word: he hadn't touched the one plant that mattered. But which one was that?

Pat picked a likely-looking plant, and began to dig.

Nothing.

He tried another, but still no gold. He kept on digging until night fell, and the moon came up. At last he went home, exhausted. Next morning, he was back, digging again, and every day after that. But as fast as he cleared a patch of ragwort, more sprang up behind him, each with a handkerchief tied round it.

Pat lived to be an old, old man, but though he kept on digging, he never did find that leprechaun's store of gold. Since the one-shoemaker gave his word that the gold was there, then it must be lying there still. But I wouldn't be trying too hard to find it, if I were you. You could be digging, like poor Pat, till your dying day.

Raven Boy

Canadian

Who is Raven Boy? What is he? He looks just like an ordinary boy. But Raven Boy can be a hare, white on white against the arctic snows. Raven Boy can be a single needle, hanging on the tallest pine tree. Best of all, Raven Boy can soar on raven's wings, over the land and the sea.

When he was young, nobody knew all the things that Raven Boy could do. He wasn't even sure himself, but he was learning, day by day.

When Raven Boy sat carving fishes out of bone, nobody saw that after he dropped the bone fish into the water, they flipped their tails and swam away.

One day, as Raven Boy sat whittling a toy canoe out of wood, his uncle called to him:

"Come fishing with me, Raven Boy," he said.

Raven Boy looked his uncle up and down. The man made him think of a grizzly bear. *"Come let me hug you! Hug you to death!"*

"All right," said Raven Boy. "I'll come fishing."

He tucked the toy canoe inside his coat.

His mother was afraid. To the uncle she said:

"Four sons I had. Now three of them are dead. Don't take the youngest from me."

"They were stupid, clumsy boys," said the uncle. He smiled at Raven Boy, and his smile was the smile of a shark that seeks its dinner. "But you are different, aren't you?"

"Oh yes," nodded Raven Boy. "I am different. Don't worry, Mother, I'll be back!"

So Raven Boy set out with his uncle, and when their canoe was out of sight of land, he asked: "Why did you kill my brothers?"

"How do you know I killed them?"

"I just know," said Raven Boy. "Why did you do it?"

The uncle shrugged. "It's just my nature, I suppose. I hate boys. One I killed with my club, because he was stupid, the second I killed with my spear because he was slow. The third fell asleep, so I left him on the ice for the polar bears to eat. You, you ask too many questions. I think I'll feed you to the fishes."

And so saying, the uncle picked the boy up by his heels, and tipped him into the icy water. Down, down, down went Raven Boy, holding his breath until his lungs were bursting. He kicked with his feet, but the weight of his boots still carried him downwards. So he took them off, and his coat, too, but he still hung on to the little canoe he had made. Why had he brought it? He didn't know. He must let his breath out soon, or he would surely burst.

As Raven Boy breathed out over the little canoe, it began to grow. The more he breathed out, the bigger and lighter it grew, until at last it was able to carry him to the surface of the sea. By this time it was big enough for a boy to ride in, so Raven Boy climbed in, and set off after his uncle. He had no paddle, but he was Raven Boy, and the little boat skimmed along, all by itself, over the tops of the waves.

"Have you seen my uncle?" he asked the gulls.

"Aaark!" they screamed back. "This way."

"Have you seen my uncle?" he called to the dolphins.

"A man with a spear?" they asked him.

"That's right, that's him. Did he come this way?"

The dolphins did not answer, but dived underneath the boat. Raven Boy felt a thump, and the canoe split in two. Down he tumbled, right to the very bottom of the sea.

"Why did you do that?" Raven Boy yelled at the dolphins. "I've never done you any harm."

He was so angry he said it without thinking, and to his surprise, he found he could breathe and talk quite normally, and he followed the dolphins to where a young one lay with a fishing spear in his side. He was close to death.

"Your uncle speared him," said the dolphins. "If he dies, then you die too. A life for a life, that is our law."

Raven Boy looked at the dying dolphin. He thought of the bone fish that had come to life as he dropped them in the water. Could he bring back life from the very edge of death? He didn't know. He had never tried.

But one thing he did know. "Your brother will drown if he doesn't have air to breathe," he said.

He told the dolphins to carry their wounded brother up to the air and the light. When they reached the surface, he took hold of the spear, and pulled it out. He held ice against the wound to stop the bleeding, and he whispered to the young dolphin:

"If you die, then so must I. But if you live, then I will seek out my uncle who tried to kill us both. If I have to go to the end of the world to find him, I will make him pay for what he has done. So please live, dolphin, please live!"

Under his fingers' touch, he felt the young dolphin's heart begin to beat more strongly, and he knew that it would live. And so would he.

Raven Boy stayed with the dolphins for many days, learning their language and singing their songs until the young dolphin was well again. Then the dolphin school brought Raven Boy to the seashore, not far from his own village.

"Thank you, Raven Boy," they called to him, as they swam out to sea. "If ever you need us, call us. Call us, and we will be there!"

And with a flick of their tails and a somersault or two, they were gone.

Raven Boy travelled home on his raven's wings. You can imagine how pleased his people were to see him.

"We thought you were dead," said his mother. "Your uncle said you had fallen overboard."

"He pushed me," said Raven Boy. "He tried to kill me, as he killed my brothers."

He looked round angrily for his uncle. "Where is he?"

But his uncle was nowhere to be found. He kept hidden from Raven Boy for a very long time – right up to the day when...

But that's another story!

The Terrible Dibdib

Arabian

Ali was a thief, but it wasn't really his fault. If God had made him the son of a carpenter, he would have been a happy carpenter. But God had chosen to make him the son of a thief, so he went into the family business. It wasn't much of a business. Rich people put bars and shutters on their windows and doors, and the rest were no better off than Ali himself. But on hot summer nights, when windows were left open, Ali would reach in and help himself to a loaf of bread or a few odd coins, or whatever came to hand.

One night, Ali was reaching in at the window of an old woman's house, feeling about for whatever he could find, when a voice spoke out of the darkness.

"Oooh! Oooh! Did ever a poor woman suffer so! This terrible dibdib will be the death of me! I've done everything I can, but there's no cure. Dibdib! Dibdib! I can't live through another night of it!"

Ali stood frozen to the spot. Dibdib? Was it some sort of illness? It sounded terrible! Dibdib! How did you catch it? Maybe just by breathing in the same air! He had been standing here much too long. He could feel himself breaking out in a cold sweat already!

Ali hurried home as fast as he could, though his legs were having trouble

holding him up, and he kept bumping into things.

"You're back early," said his wife as he arrived. "What have you got for us, then?"

"Dibdib!" moaned Ali. "The terrible dibdib, that's what I've got! Keep away! Send for the doctor! I think I'm going to die!"

Much alarmed, his wife fetched the doctor.

"He says he's got the dibdib, doctor. Is it very catching?"

The doctor was supposed to have a cure for everything. He wasn't going to admit that he had never heard of such an illness. He looked very grave, and Ali, looking up at him from his bed, thought: "Oh my goodness, it is bad! I am going to die!"

"There, there," said the doctor, thinking that if there was a new illness about, he should find out something about it. "Where exactly do you think you picked up this – er – touch of the dibdib?"

"At an old woman's house," said Ali. "I was just passing by and happened to – er – look in at the window, to see if she'd left anything about that might get stolen. There are some terrible thieves about, doctor!"

"I know," said the doctor, who had recently mislaid a rather nice coffee pot (with the coffee still in it), and a plateful of Turkish delight.

Off went the doctor to the old woman's house. Should he go in? What if he caught the dibdib himself? What if he died of it? He stood outside the window and listened.

"Oooh!" moaned the old woman. "Oooh! Won't someone put me out of my

misery! I can't stand this terrible dibdib any longer!"

Then she suddenly sat up in bed. "Who's there?" she demanded, for she had seen the figure at the window. "You ought to be ashamed of yourself – peering in at people's windows in the middle of the night, scaring them silly!"

She didn't seem very ill. The doctor felt a bit braver.

"I've come about the terrible dibdib," he said.

"Oh," said the old woman. "Are you a plumber?"

"No, I'm a doctor."

"What do I want a doctor for?" she snapped. "I'm not ill."

"Not ill! What about the terrible dibdib?"

"The terrible dibdib! The terrible dibdib!" The old woman began to laugh. "There's your terrible dibdib!"

She pointed to the water-tap in the corner. "Listen!"

The tap was dripping steadily into the sink. *Dibdib, dibdib, dibdib.*

"All night long it keeps me awake. *Dibdib, dibdib!* Cure that if you can, doctor!"

The doctor felt very silly, but when he arrived back at Ali's house, he was wearing his gravest face again.

"I can cure you of the dibdib, Ali," he said. "But it won't be easy."

Ali began moaning. "I'm a poor man, doctor –"

"You're a thief," said the doctor. "And if you're going to stay a thief for the rest of your days, I'm not sure it wouldn't be best to let you die now!"

"Thieving's my trade, doctor. What else can I do?"

"Anything you like," said the doctor. "It's bound to be better than dying of the terrible dibdib."

"All right, I'll give it up, I promise you."

The doctor gave him a cup of water, and Ali sat up and drank it.

"Doctor, it's a miracle! I feel better already!" he cried.

"Good," said the doctor. But the real miracle would be, he thought, if Ali really did manage to give up his thieving ways.

Surprisingly enough, Ali kept his word. He became a handyman, fixing this and that. He found he liked the work. Plenty of fresh air and sunshine, and grateful people to talk to. In time, they became his friends. One of his first jobs was to fix a leaky tap for a certain old lady. She told Ali that the doctor had advised her to call him.

So perhaps that doctor did have a cure for everything – even for the terrible dibdib!

The Great Rain

Native American

The earth is our mother. She gives us food. She gives us shelter. She gives us beauty, all around. In beauty we walk every day, close to our mother, the earth. Earth Mother is very easy to love. But where would she be without our father, the sky, who sends the sun and the rain? She would be nothing but a barren desert.

Sky Father is not so easy to love. The sky is so very far away.

Sky Father grew jealous of Earth Mother. He grew very angry.

"I will show them all I do for them! I will make them notice me!" he roared.

Every day Sky Father made the sun shine, hotter and hotter. The streams dried up, the land began to die, and all the creatures of the world hid themselves in the shadows, away from the terrible heat of the sun.

Earth Mother went to Sky Father and begged him:

"Let it rain soon. Without rain, all the creatures of the world will die."

Sky Father was still angry.

"They want rain, do they?" he shouted. "I'll send them rain. I'll send them more rain than has ever fallen since the beginning of the world!"

"Why then," said Earth Mother, "the world will flood, and everyone will still die."

"And serve them right!" cried Sky Father.

Earth Mother sighed. There was no reasoning with him in this mood. "He can't flood everything," she told herself. "Not the hills and the mountain tops, too."

Earth Mother went swiftly about the world, walking, walking, telling every creature that the flood was coming.

The bison heard her, and the wolf, the coyote and the prairie dog.

All the animals heard her warning, and headed for the hills.

To the hunter she whispered:

"The flood is coming. Take your family and go to the mountains."

But the hunter heard only the sighing of the wind through the dry grasses.

Earth Mother murmured her warning to the woman searching for shellfish in the mud of the shrinking river-bed, but the woman heard only the chattering of water over pebbles.

"They have forgotten my voice," thought Earth Mother. "It is only their own language they understand now."

So she changed herself into an old, old woman, and she went walking, walking from village to village, warning everyone:

"The flood is coming. Save yourselves and your children. Go!"

The people heard her. They packed up their tepees and blankets and cooking pots and set off for the mountains.

Earth Mother went on walking, until she came to a village where all the people were dancing, shaking gourd rattles filled with seeds, and sticks with shells nailed to them.

"The rain is coming," she told them.

"We know that, you stupid old woman. The rain is coming, because we are dancing a rain-dance."

Earth Mother said: "You don't understand. This time there will be more rain than has ever fallen since the beginning of the world. You will all be drowned if you stay here."

They didn't believe her. They hissed at her, and stuck out their tongues,

waggled their bottoms, and pushed her so she fell down. They kicked sand in her face, and went on dancing, and shaking their rattles, and making the sound of the rain.

"The rain is coming!" they cried. "The rain is coming because we are dancing!"

Already the clouds were gathering in the sky.

Earth Mother loves all her children. Even the naughty ones. Even the ones who hurt her.

She was determined to save them if she could.

The dancers danced on, their bodies swaying from side to side across the sand, until they began to find that their legs weren't strong enough to hold them upright.

Still those naughty children went on trying to dance, wriggling on their bellies across the sand, shaking their rattles.

Earth Mother had changed them all into rattle snakes.

She picked them up, one by one, coiled them neatly round her arm, and popped them in her basket. Then she carried them to safety in the high places, just as the first drops of rain began to fall.

How it rained! The thunder crashed and lightning flashed and the rain poured down from the sky. Day after day it fell, filling the streams and the forests, right up to the tallest tree-tops.

The creatures on the high mountains, though, they were safe from harm. At last, Sky Father's anger was quite worn out. The sun came out and the waters slowly went down again. As the days went by, the people could see the tops of

the hills, then the forest trees, and the rocks and the great plains.

The creatures and the people all went back to their homes.

As for the rattle snakes, as soon as Earth Mother let them out of her basket, they slithered away into the shadows. They were ashamed of themselves, and a bit afraid, too.

Ever since that time, rattle snakes have crept along, keeping close to the Earth Mother. Sometimes, they look up at the sky and shake their rattles.

"Is it raining? If it does, you will look after us, Earth Mother?"

Earth Mother smiles. Like any other mother, she loves all her children, even the naughty ones.

The Big White Cat

Scandinavian

Trolls! I never heard of anyone with a good word to say for them. The big ones will knock you down and sit on your head, just by way of saying "Good morning". The little ones are far worse. There's only one thing to do with a troll, and that is to lure him out into the sunlight. A touch of the sun will turn a troll to stone, and he'll give you no more trouble. But trolls know that, of course.

So they live in the far, far north, where the winter nights are longest. All summer, they sleep deep underground. Then, with the first snows, they come creeping out to see what mischief they can do.

It was snowing now, snow on snow. Through it, a man was walking. Nils Nilsson was his name. Close behind him came an animal, white against the white snow. What was it? A dog? No, a bear, a great, white polar bear.

Nils wasn't afraid. He knew the bear was there. They were friends, the bear and he, ever since Nils had found him as a cub, all alone on the ice. The bear kept him company on his travels. Sometimes it was hard to find a place to stay, with a bear in tow, but most people were kind when they saw how gentle he was.

The snow was falling thickly now, and Nils knew they must find a place to stay very soon. Then, in the distance, Nils saw an inn. As he approached, he saw that the shutters were closed, and the inn keeper was loading his bag on to a

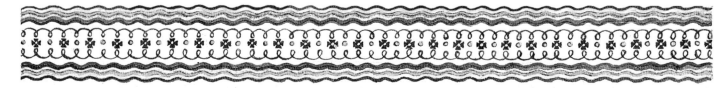

sledge. "Where are you going?" asked Nils.

"I'm off to stay at an inn," said the inn keeper.

"But this *is* an inn," said Nils. "It's your inn. Why don't you stay here?"

"Never!" said the inn keeper, shuddering. "No one else wants to, either."

"I do," said Nils.

"Help yourself," said the inn keeper. "Take any room. Take the whole place! I don't want it."

"Thank you very much," said Nils.

"Just don't say I didn't warn you." Off went the inn keeper, pulling his sledge along behind him, before Nils could ask: "Warn me about what?"

Nils and the bear went inside. Very nice it was too, with a stack of logs for the fire, and a larder full of food. They cooked themselves a meal, and then sat toasting their toes by the fire.

The bear was curled up fast asleep when Nils got the first hint of trouble – a scritch-scritch-scratching in the wainscot.

Then came a tap-tapping at the door. Poor Nils lost count of the number of times he went to open it, only to find no one there.

Next, came a pitter-pattering of footsteps up and down stairs, and a deep chuckling from inside the chimney. Then they began to show themselves...

Trolls!

Sliding under the door they came, swinging down from the rafters, creeping up through the cracks between the floorboards, and riding down the chimney on a puff of smoke. They smashed the plates and splattered the left-over food all over the walls. They pulled Nils Nilsson's hair, and tweaked his nose, and pinched him in all the places where it hurts most. They put a spider down his neck, and when he stood up to shake it out, he found they had tied his shoelaces together.

Down he went, Crash, Bang, Thump! The bear stirred in his sleep, and began to snore. "Ooh!" cried the trolls. "What's this?"

Nils smiled. "That? It's just my cat. Don't disturb her now, or you'll be sorry."

"Ahhh!" cried the trolls. "We like to play with cats! Here, pussy, pussy, pussy!" They jumped on the bear, and tugged his ears. "Nice pussy! Here, have some milk!" And they emptied the milk jug over his head.

At last the bear woke up. Slowly he stretched himself. Splat! went one paw, with a troll concertina'd underneath. Swish! went the other paw, and a couple more trolls went sailing through the air.

The bear stood up, and half the trolls on his back tumbled off amongst the ashes of the fire. The rest were carried higher and higher, their bony fingers scrabbling to hold on. Very itchy! The bear strolled over and rubbed his back up and down against the doorpost, until he had scratched them all off. Then he looked around in some surprise at the trolls scattered round him on the floor, rubbing their cuts and bruises and their aching heads.

He was a friendly bear, always ready to make new friends. And so he smiled, showing his sharp white teeth.

"Aaagh!" screamed the trolls. "Pussy cat's going to eat us!"

They made for the doors, the windows, the chimney, and squeezed themselves down the cracks in the floorboards. In a few minutes, there wasn't a troll to be

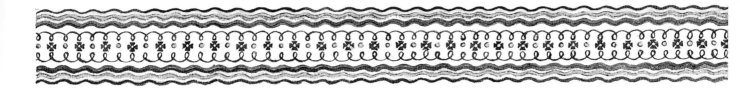

seen or heard anywhere – not that night, nor any other night, for the rest of the winter. The inn keeper never returned, so Nils stayed on. There were plenty of customers again, once word had got round that the trolls were gone.

Summer came round again, and autumn. The days were getting shorter, and Nils was clearing the first snow away from his front door, when he heard a voice calling from among the forest trees. "Nils! Nils Nilsson!"

"That's me," said Nils. He recognised the voice at once. A troll's voice, once heard, is not something you forget.

"We're looking for a place to spend the winter, Nils."

Nils smiled. "You can come to my place, and welcome. My cat will be glad of the company."

"Oooooooh!" There was a hurried whispering among the trees, then:

"You still got that big, white pussy cat?"

"I have," said Nils. "I shouldn't be surprised if she doesn't have some kittens soon – six or seven at the least."

There was another whispering among the trees. Then silence.

"When shall we expect you then?" called Nils.

But there was no reply – just a pattering of little feet, moving away, very fast.

To make sure those trolls had gone for good this time, Nils had a sign painted to hang outside, with the name of the inn in big letters.

What do you think he called it? Why, The White Cat, of course!

Stone Soup

English

The Storyteller came over the hill, an ostrich feather in his hat and his scarlet cloak a-billowing in the wind. He knocked on the door of the first house he came to. "Spare me a bite to eat," he said, "and I'll tell you a story."

"No, thank you, we don't need stories," said the woman.

"But Mother –" said Peter.

Too late. The door was shut in the Storyteller's face.

Off went the Storyteller to the next house. Peter would have liked to hear a story, and so he followed a little way behind.

Knock, knock!

"Do you want any stories today?"

Emily would have liked a story, too, but her mother said:

"Not today, thank you."

Someone might like a story, thought Emily, and she slipped out and followed Peter down the street.

All round the village the Storyteller went, knocking on every door. No one would give him a bite to eat. No grown up wanted his stories, only the children. In twos and threes, from every house, they followed him. Not too close though, for he was a stranger, and they had been told not to talk to strangers.

They came just near enough to hear if anyone asked for a story. But no one did. The Storyteller heaved a big sigh. "Looks like I'll be eating stone soup again," he said to the world in general.

There on the village green he built a little fire of sticks. From somewhere under his scarlet cloak he took out a billy-can. He filled it with water and set it on the fire to boil. Then he began to wander up and down, eyes on the ground, as if he was searching for something. As he went, he muttered to himself, just loud enough for the children to hear:

> *"This one's too big and that one's too small,*
> *That one's too knobbly – it won't do at all.*
> *This one's too dark and t'other's too light,*
> *But this over here? This one is just right!"*

In his hand he held a large, flat stone. He dusted it, blew on it, washed it carefully, and popped it into the billy-can.

"Stone soup," said the Storyteller. "Delicious!"

He sat on the ground, waiting for the water to boil. Round him, in a circle, sat the children – not too close, for he was still a stranger. Stone soup? they wondered. Whoever had heard of making soup from a stone?

Soon the water was bubbling away. From somewhere under his scarlet cloak the Storyteller took out a spoon. He ladled a spoonful of the boiling water, blew on it to cool it, and tasted it.

"Mm," he said to himself. "It's coming along nicely. What it could do with now is just a pinch of salt."

Without a word, Emily jumped up, raced home, and came back with a pinch of salt. She gave it to the Storyteller, and the Storyteller put it in the billy-can. They all watched while he tasted the soup again.

"Much better," he decided. "It would be better still if I only had a little bit of meat."

Off ran Peter to fetch that spare piece of bacon from the larder. Into the billy-can it went. Still the Storyteller sat, and the children all watched him.

He tasted the soup again.

"Stone soup!" he said. "I can hardly wait! Though a bit of onion would make all the difference."

In less time than it takes to tell, there was the onion simmering away in the billy-can.

Still the Storyteller sat. Each time he tasted the soup, it was almost ready – but not quite. It needed just a touch of carrot...a few peas...a tomato...a handful of barley...

Each time the children rushed off home to fetch them. By now they all wanted to make stone soup.

At last the Storyteller gave the soup a final stir and tasted it one last time.

"Stone soup," he said. "Delicious!"

It certainly smelt delicious. Who would have thought that stone soup would smell so good?

The Storyteller took the billy-can off the fire and blew on the soup to cool it. Then he drank the soup and spooned up the vegetables, the barley and the

bacon, until there was nothing left but the stone. He fished it out, and threw it away.

"I don't need that," he said, "and I never did."

Then he took off his feathered hat and bowed to left and right.

"Fair's fair," he said. "I've had a bite to eat and you've had a story."

"What story?" asked Peter.

"Stone soup," said the Storyteller, grinning, and off he went, over the next hill, with his scarlet cloak a-billowing in the wind, while all the children ran home to teach their mothers how to make stone soup.

The Smallest Boy in the World

Japanese

His name was Timimoto, and if he had been any smaller, he wouldn't have been there at all. He was just five centimetres tall, from his head to his toes, but his parents loved him just as much as if he had been a full sized boy. "He'll grow when he's ready," his father said. "Meanwhile, he is very cheap to feed."

His mother said: "He's so easy to look after! I just pop him into my pocket."

But it was not long before Timimoto became tired of living in his mother's pocket, and started tumbling out.

"Just mind you don't fall into the milk," his mother warned him. "At least not until you've learned to swim."

Timimoto was more careful after that, and would climb down his mother's skirts to the floor. Once there, he was as mischievous as any other boy. He drove the hens wild, by riding their chicks all round the yard, and round the kitchen, too. A cat mistook him for a mouse once, but she soon discovered her mistake. Mice don't punch you on the nose, yelling: "Put me down, you great moth-eaten rug!"

The cat dropped him, but it was a narrow escape. After that, Timimoto took his mother's darning-needle, and wore it like a sword.

One day, he discovered the stream at the bottom of the garden, and he borrowed his father's rice bowl for a boat, punting himself along with a chopstick. His parents refused to fuss about him, just because he was small. "Boys like to have adventures," they said. But they did not know at that time

of the big adventure in store for their tiny son.

It all began one hot, sunny day. Timimoto was sprawled, half asleep, in his rice bowl boat among the rushes. But as he slept, it rained hard, high in the mountains above him, and a huge torrent of water came pouring down the river into the stream, sweeping Timimoto away. When he awoke, he found his little rice bowl spinning round and round in the raging water of the big river. It was too deep for him to reach the bottom with his chopstick.

By dinnertime, Timimoto was far, far away, spinning down the river towards the sea. Boats passed by, but nobody saw him until the rice bowl bobbed right up against a ferryboat that was crossing the river. The ferryman fished it out of the water, and found Timimoto.

"Well, well," he said. "Who are you?"

"I'm Timimoto, the smallest boy in the world. You must have heard of me – everyone in the village knows who I am."

"Ah, but this isn't a village," said the ferryman. "This is a town."

From the ferryboat Timimoto saw the shore, and what he saw amazed him. There were no fields, no trees, no birds or animals. There were huge buildings everywhere he looked – and people! There were hundreds and hundreds of them!

"Will you take me there, please?" Timimoto begged the ferryman, and the ferryman agreed.

"Mind you don't get stepped on," he warned Timimoto, as he put him ashore. "And don't stay out after dark, or the ogre will eat you!"

"Ogre, what ogre?" cried Timimoto, as the ferryman pulled away from the shore.

"One that eats people," the ferryman shouted back.

Ogres are a kind of giant. Timimoto knew that, from the stories his mother told him. Everyone was a giant to Timimoto, and he wasn't afraid of them. As for eating people, no giant would touch him, for he would hardly make a mouthful. All the same, Timimoto put a hand to his side to make sure his darning needle sword was still there.

As darkness fell, all the people of the town scurried homewards to lock their doors and windows. Far out to sea, a great wave of water was tumbling towards the shore. After it a figure strode, roaring as it came, all covered in barnacles and hung with seaweed, a crest of spines down its back, and one red eye in the middle of its forehead.

"So that's an ogre," said Timimoto, more interested than frightened.

The great wave broke on the seashore, and a tide of water flowed through the streets, leaving in its wake, dead fish and crabs and seaweed. Timimoto was picked up by the water, and carried down to the edge of the sea, just as the ogre stepped out of it.

"WHERE'S MY DINNER?" roared the ogre, stamping his feet and flattening three fishing boats drawn up on the sand. "I WANT MEAT! MAN MEAT!"

He flung out his arm, and a house collapsed like a pack of cards. The ogre began to search among the ruins for some man meat.

"Stop that!" cried Timimoto, jabbing at the ogre's finger with his sword.

"Ow!" yelled the ogre.

"Go back to where you came from, you great bully," shouted Timimoto, stabbing at the monster's big toe.

"Ouch!" cried the ogre. "Mosquitoes!"

Timimoto dug in his sword and held on to it for dear life, as the ogre lifted his foot to scratch it, resting it on his knee. Timimoto jabbed the knee, too, then he moved quickly on, before the ogre's hand could squash him flat. Up and up the ogre's body he climbed, using the seaweed as a rope, and stepping from barnacle to barnacle, jabbing as he went.

The ogre forgot all about his dinner. Mosquitoes, they seemed to be everywhere! He danced about and waved his arms, and slapped himself wherever he felt a sting. Then he heard a humming noise, like a tiny voice.

"You're just a great bag of wind, aren't you? I'm not scared of you!"

That was no mosquito! What was it, then? "Who are you?" yelled the ogre.

"I'm Timimoto, the smallest boy in the world!"

The ogre swatted his neck so hard, he nearly knocked himself over, but Timimoto dodged the blow, and climbed even higher.

The ogre narrowed his one eye, and looked around, but he couldn't see the top of his own head. There stood Timimoto, gripping his needle sword in both hands. There was his target – the ogre's eye! Timimoto thrust in the sword with all his might.

The ogre fell, stone dead – but not like a stone. It was more like the crumpling of a balloon, with a slow hissing from between his teeth. As the ogre breathed his last breath, Timimoto gave a great sigh of relief.

A very strange thing began to happen then. Timimoto started to grow. Before he realised what was happening, he was half a metre tall, and still growing. Three quarters, one metre, one and a half, one and three quarters –

"Oh no," cried Timimoto. "I don't want to be a giant."

He shut his mouth, and pinched his nose for as long as he could.

When he finally drew breath again, he stayed as he was – nearly two metres tall, a very fine young man, and a rich one too, because of course there was a reward for ridding the town of that ogre.

Timimoto made his way home, up the river and along the stream. His parents could hardly believe their eyes.

"Timimoto, is it really you?" His mother didn't know whether to laugh or cry or scold him for going off without a word and losing his father's rice bowl.

As for Timimoto's father, when he could get a word in, all he said was:

"Didn't I always say he would grow when he was ready?"

The King with Dusty Feet

Indian

Long ago and far away there lived a king who never took a bath. Never? No, never. Didn't he smell? Of course he did. He smelt terrible. But nobody dared tell him so, because he was the King. His courtiers held their breath when he came too close, and if he wasn't looking, they held their noses too. As he travelled round his kingdom with his courtiers and his servants, his soldiers and his elephants, people were too impressed by the splendour of it all to notice the bad smell, or, if they did, they blamed it on the elephants.

One day, the King came to a village he had never visited before. A little girl was chosen to present the King with a garland of flowers. The King smiled in a kingly way as she hung the garland round his neck. But the little girl didn't smile back. She screwed up her face and wrinkled her nose.

"Pooh!" she said. "You smell!"

She said it so loudly and so clearly that nobody could pretend they hadn't heard. Her mother rushed forward to drag her away. "Silly girl," she said. "It's the King. A king never smells!"

"Yes he does," said the little girl. "He smells awful. Don't you ever take a bath?" she asked him.

"No," said the King. "Of course I don't."

He asked the courtier standing nearest him. "Do *you* ever take a bath?"

The courtier had to admit that he did – quite often.

The King asked another: "Do you ever take a bath?"

"Er – sometimes," stammered the courtier.

Then the King asked everyone the same question, the courtiers and the soldiers and the servants. And the reply was always the same. All of them took baths.

The King began to feel quite left out.

"Today," he said grandly, "I will take a bath. Here and now. In the river."

Such a to-do there was then, finding soaps and sponges and towels and talcum powder fit for a king to use, and putting up screens, so that he could have his bath in private.

Everyone held their breath as the King stepped into the water. After a moment, they heard singing from behind the screens, as the river carried the first soapsuds away.

"I must do this again some time," said the King, as he emerged from the river, dried himself and put on some nice, clean clothes. "Perhaps next year."

Then he noticed his feet. They were dirty again. Of course they were, for the King was standing on the dusty river bank.

The King stepped back into the water, washed his feet again, and came back on to the river bank to dry them. He had not taken more than a few steps, when once more, his feet were covered in dust.

"This river bank is dirty," said the King. "Clean it immediately!"

Everyone fetched buckets of water and scrubbing brushes and brooms, and they worked away on the river bank, while the King stood in the river, waiting

till they had finished. But when he stepped on to dry land again, his feet became dirtier than ever, because by now the bank was muddy and wet.

Back into the river he went, then out again. In again. And out again. And he would probably be doing this still if the little girl who had caused all the trouble hadn't gone running off home to fetch her mother's best goatskin rug. She spread it out on the river bank for the King to stand on.

The King took one step, then another, then three, four, five and six. His feet were still clean, but he had run out of rug.

All the villagers went hurrying off to fetch rugs and blankets and shawls, and somehow they managed to make a path for the King to walk on all the way back to the palace.

That was all well and good. But a path of rugs and shawls from the palace to the river bank was not enough. The King wished to visit the rest of his kingdom.

"I want the whole land covered in a leather carpet, so that my feet will stay clean wherever I go," he decreed.

Now everywhere he went his feet *did* stay clean – but nobody seemed pleased to see him any more. Nobody waved as he passed by with his courtiers and his servants, his soldiers and his elephants (all with beautifully clean feet). Nobody cheered. They just looked sad.

A year passed, and the King went back to the river for another bath.

Nobody was there to see him, but one little girl (and you can guess who that was).

"What's the matter with everyone?" asked the King. "I don't smell any more, do I?"

"Only a bit," said the little girl. It was a whole year, after all, since the King's last bath.

"Why do they all look so sad, then?"

"Because they have nothing to eat," said the little girl. "You've covered the land with a carpet of leather, so that nothing can grow."

"Oh," said the King. He looked down at his nice clean feet. "What can I do then? I don't want to go around with dirty feet."

The little girl sighed. "It's just as well *I* know what to do, isn't it?"

She went home and fetched her mother's scissors. When she came back she cut through the leather all round the King's left foot, and all round his right. She tied the pieces of leather to his feet with leather laces, and she tied the laces round his ankles.

"There you are," she said. "Now you have your own bit of carpet to keep your feet clean wherever you go."

And that is how the first pair of shoes came to be made. Soon everyone was wearing them. Well, they had to find a use for all that leather, didn't they?

The Fox and the Rooster

French

He's a fine fellow, is Raynard the fox. He is smart as paint, with his sleek, russet coat and bushy tail, bright eyes and sharp, white teeth. To Partlet the hen, of course, those eyes meant just one thing. Dinner! Poor Partlet! Every night she saw old Raynard, prowling through her dreams, and she would wake up, all of a flutter.

"There, there," said her husband, Chanticleer. "Don't be afraid. I'll look after you."

"It's not me he wants," clucked Partlet. "It's you!"

Chanticleer shook his head scornfully. "It was just a dream."

"But what if it was an awful warning? What if it comes true?"

"Silly bird!" Chanticleer gave her a peck on the cheek. "What could possibly happen to me, here in the farmyard? Now, no more talk of Raynard and chicken dinners. I have work to do. I must wake the sun so that the day can begin."

Off strutted Chanticleer, across the yard. He took a quick look at his reflection in the pond, to make sure that every feather was in place. Then he hopped up to the top of the dunghill, and crowed

till the hills echoed with the sound and the sun peeped sleepily over the horizon. When the farmer's wife came out to feed the chickens, he hopped down again, to organise the pecking order.

"Why does Partlet always have to be first?" the other hens complained.

"Because she lays the most eggs," said Chanticleer.

"Of course she does!" they fussed. "She gets the most to eat!"

By the time Chanticleer had had his own breakfast, he was ready for a rest in the haystore. And it was there that he saw a pair of bright eyes, staring at him, and the gleam of sharp, white teeth.

Raynard the fox! Just as Partlet had seen him in her dreams!

Chanticleer lifted his head and raised the alarm.

At once Raynard sat up, and cried:

"Oh, please sing again!"

Chanticleer put his head to one side.

"Don't you want to eat me?" he asked.

"Eat you!" cried Raynard. "There's more to my life than eating and sleeping. I love the scent of flowers, and the dancing of the butterflies. But best of all, I love the song you sing to wake the world each morning."

"Really?" Chanticleer preened himself.

"I admire you so much. Please sing for me!"

"Stay where you are, then. Don't come any closer."

"I won't." Raynard settled down, with his chin on his paws. Enough meat there for three days at the very least, he was thinking, as Chanticleer puffed out his chest and began to crow. Suddenly he stopped.

"You moved!" Chanticleer said.

"Did I?" said Raynard, surprised. "I'm sorry. Please go on."

And stretching out his neck, Chanticleer began his song again.

Slowly, slowly, by shuffling his back legs, Raynard edged closer, but he still wasn't close enough.

"Beautiful!" he sighed, when the song was over.

"Did you really like it?"

"I've never heard any bird sing like it," Raynard said. "Except perhaps..."

"Except who?" demanded Chanticleer.

"Your dear father, of course. I can see him now. He used to stretch out his neck, just as you do. And then, when he began to sing, he would close his eyes! That was what turned his voice from the voice of a rooster to the voice of an angel."

I'll just close one eye, thought Chanticleer, and see if it makes a difference.

And oh, it did! He could tell that from the eager look on Raynard's face. Chanticleer sang on, reaching for the top note – the one he had never reached in his life before. He never made it. The moment he shut his other eye, Raynard had him by the throat.

Chanticleer's song ended with a strangled squawk, and Raynard was off across the farmyard, with the rooster in his mouth.

"It's him!" screamed Partlet. "Just as in my dream!"

The rest of the hens squawked and clucked and ran about until the farmer came out, just in time to see Raynard leap the fence, with Chanticleer between his teeth. The farmer whistled up his dogs and set off after them, without much hope of catching up.

Poor Chanticleer could hardly breathe.

"Must you hold me quite so tightly?" he wheezed.

Raynard knew better than to open his mouth to answer. He ran on.

"Who is going to wake the sun up in the morning, if I'm not there to do it? Who is going to keep those hens in order? Oh, poor Partlet. I suppose you wouldn't consider letting me go?"

Still no answer. Raynard ran on.

"Is this how you caught my father, too?" he asked. Silence.

Chanticleer peered over Raynard's shoulder to see if the farmer and his dogs were catching up at all, but there was no hope there – no hope at all.

"Oh well," sighed Chanticleer, "you got the better of me, fair and square, and I deserve to be eaten. I wish you could see that farmer! He is miles behind, shaking his fist. Why don't you tell him what a fool he looks? 'Give up, old man! Go home and count your chickens' – something like that."

Raynard thought of all the times the farmer and his dogs had chased him away. Oh, but he'd got the better of them now, and he would tell them so. He felt quite safe, and his dinner was as good as inside him. "Oh, I'm Raynard the fox," he would say. "A very fine fellow indeed!"

He opened his mouth – and Chanticleer spread his wings and fluttered up into the branches of the nearest tree.

"Come down!" cried Raynard.

"Come down and be eaten?" crowed Chanticleer. "No, thank you!"

"You said I'd got the better of you and you deserved to be eaten," said Raynard.

"Did I? Well, now I've got the better of *you*! I suppose there's a moral in this for us both. Never close your eyes when they should be open – and never open your mouth when it should be shut!"

A Song for Hinemoa

New Zealand

Lovely as the moon was Hinemoa, gentle as the summer rain, her voice soft as the wind whispering through the trees. Many men asked to marry her, many warriors, many chiefs, but her father sent them all away. No man was good enough for his daughter, Hinemoa. No man? Perhaps one.

Tutanekai came from across the water to the gathering of the tribes, and Hinemoa loved him at first sight. But every time she looked at him, Tutanekai was careful to be looking somewhere else. He did not dare to ask to marry Hinemoa, in case her father sent him away like the rest. If that happened, then he knew his life would be dust and ashes for ever.

When the gathering of the tribes was over, Tutanekai went back to his own people across the water. He made himself a flute to play out of a hollow reed. Into his music he put all his love and longing for Hinemoa the beautiful.

Softly, through the evening mist, the song of the flute came stealing across the lake to Hinemoa's people. Men, women and little children all stopped to listen, feeling both happy and sad at the same time, without knowing why.

Hinemoa alone understood the message in the music:

> *Hinemoa, my love is yours. My life is yours.*
> *Without you, my life is dust and ashes.*

Who was the flute player? Hinemoa did not know. The music called to her as on and on it played, far into the night.

When everyone was sound asleep, Hinemoa crept down to the beach. She slipped out of her clothes and into the water, and she began to swim across the lake. Oh, the water was cold! As cold as death. Hinemoa's toes and fingers were soon numb, and the cold was creeping into her very bones. But on she swam, towards the farther shore. The blood was freezing in her veins, and the teeth rattling in her head, when at last she crawled out of the water.

The music had long ago faded away. "What am I doing here?" wondered Hinemoa. "I shall die of cold and loneliness, and no one will ever know why." Then, looking round, she saw in the moonlight steam rising from a pool of water fed by a hot spring. Hinemoa stepped into it. It was like a warm bath, and she began to feel her toes and fingers again. She hummed quietly to herself, trying to remember the tune that had called her across the water.

So it was that a young huntsman heard her, as he was returning to his village, long after dark. Tired as he was, he ran on the rest of the way to raise the alarm. A spirit! There was a spirit living in the pool by the hot spring. It had called out to him or, rather, it had sung, trying to lure him in, or else drive him away. Yes, that was it! All the villagers must keep away from the pool from now on.

Then Tutanekai spoke. "The pool by the hot spring is a good place. If a spirit has come to live there, we should speak gently to it, and it will do us no harm." To show them that there was nothing to be afraid of, Tutanekai went to the pool himself. Through the mist and shadows he could see that someone was

there. Softly, he called out: "Don't be afraid! Are you a spirit?"

"No," answered Hinemoa. "Are you?"

Tutanekai laughed. "No, I am Tutanekai, chief of this place. Won't you come down to the village? We will give you food and drink and a place to rest."

Hinemoa's heart leapt when she heard his name. But what would he think of her, a crazy girl who threw off her clothes and jumped into the lake, because she heard the music of a flute! She hid her face in shame as Tutanekai gave her his cloak to wrap around her, and led her to the village.

"Go back to sleep," he told his people. "There is no spirit. Only a girl."

A girl? Who is she? Where did she come from? Why does she hide her face? Is she that ugly?

As Tutanekai's people wondered about the strange girl, Hinemoa sat alone in Tutanekai's hut. She could not eat the food he had left for her. She could not sleep.

No more could Tutanekai, sitting outside alone in the moonlight, thinking of Hinemoa, far across the water. He took out his flute and, softly, he began to play:

Hinemoa, my love is yours, my life is yours...

Hinemoa thought she must have fallen asleep after all. She must be dreaming. Then she peeped outside, and saw the flute-player. It was Tutanekai.

At the same moment, Tutanekai looked up and saw Hinemoa's face, lovely as the moon.

Of course, they were married soon after that. How could Hinemoa's father say no?

The pool by the hot spring is still called Hinemoa's pool, in memory of their love.